Give

chraschka

A RICHARD JACKSON BOOK
atheneum
ATHENEUM BOOKS FOR YOUNG READERS
New York London Toronto Sydney New Delhi

ATHENEUM BOOKS FOR YOUNG READERS
An imprint of Simon & Schuster Children's Publishing Division
1230 Avenue of the Americas, New York, New York 10020

Book design by Debra Sfetsios-Conover
The text for this book is set in Basha Handwriting.
The illustrations for this book are rendered in ink and watercolor.
Manufactured in China
0614 SCP

First Edition
10 9 8 7 6 5 4 3 2 1
Library of Congress Cataloging-in-Publication Data
Raschka, Christopher, author, illustrator.
Give and take / Chris Raschka. — 1st. edition.
p. cm
"A Richard Jackson Book."
Summary: In his apple orchard, a farmer meets a little man named Take and follows his advice, which does not turn out well, and the next day meets a little man named Give, whose advice is just as bad.
ISBN 978-1-4424-1655-0
ISBN 978-1-4814-0932-2 (eBook)
[1. Decision-making—Fiction. 2. Farmers—Fiction.] I. Title.
PZ7.R1814Giv 2014
[E]—dc23
2012051503

For RJ

Every morning a farmer said to his dog, "Let us inspect the apples."

The farmer put on his hat and coat and, with a large basket on his back, he left his house by the garden gate, proceeding along a soft path to the orchard.

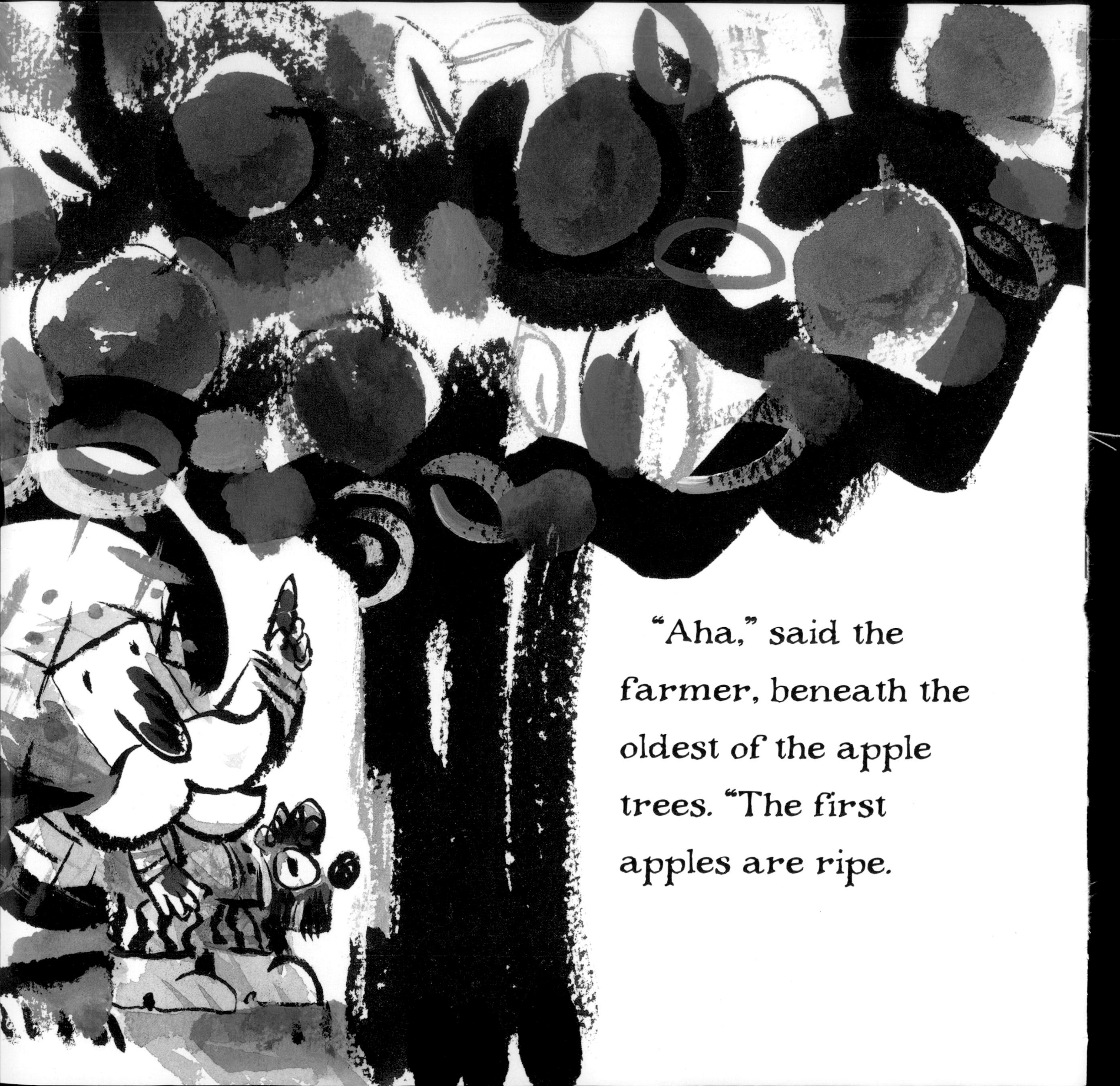

"Aha," said the farmer, beneath the oldest of the apple trees. "The first apples are ripe.

"Let us pick them."

He placed his basket at the base of the old tree and filled it with beautiful, rich red apples.

Now, as he placed the very last apple on to the top of the basket, a tiny little man leaped out at him from the bushes.

"Great Granny Smith!" said the farmer. "Who are you?"

"I am Take," the little man squeaked. "Listen to me and your life will be fine."

"But my life is fine," said the farmer.

"It will be finer," said Take.

So the farmer put him in the basket with the apples.

On the way home the farmer stopped at the house of his neighbor, who grew pumpkins.

"Hello, old man," said the neighbor.

"Hello, old woman," said the farmer.

"Would you like some pumpkins?" she said.

Now Take leaned forward and whispered in the farmer's ear, "Take them. Take all of them. Take as many as you see."

"I'll take all of them," said the farmer.

Dumping his apples out, the farmer loaded his basket with pumpkins.

"If you'll take my advice," said the old woman, "you'll make pumpkin soup."

"Take her advice, take all of it," said Take.

Thanking her, the farmer went on his way. He said, "Now what?"

"We take a hike. We take as much as we can," said the little man.

For the rest of the day, the farmer walked, the basket of pumpkins seeming to grow heavier with every step, until at last he went home. Wearily, he took the pumpkins out and then peeled and chopped and cooked them until he had gallons and gallons of pumpkin soup.

The farmer, stiff and sore, sat on his kitchen chair and thought, "I don't like pumpkin soup. It's too stringy. I wish I had an apple."

He offered the pumpkin soup to his dog, who didn't want it either, and went to bed.

The next morning the farmer
found Take asleep in the basket.
"OUT!" said the
farmer.

"Let us inspect the apples," the farmer said to his dog.

Beneath the tallest tree, the farmer said, "Ah, heavenly apples! And more are ripe!" Again he filled his basket.

Just then a tiny little man dropped out of the branches.

"Muttering Mutsus!" said the farmer. "Who are you?"

"I am Give," said the tiny man. "If you will listen to me, your life will be sweet."

"My life is sweet already," said the farmer.

"It will be sweeter," said Give.

Once more the farmer agreed, allowing Give to sit in the basket, behind his ear.

On the way home they stopped at the house of another neighbor, a pig farmer.

"My pigs would surely love to eat those apples," said the pig farmer.

The tiny man whispered, "Give him your apples. Give away everything you have."

So the farmer gave away all his apples.

"Now give him your opinions," said the tiny man. "Give away all that you have."

So the farmer shared every thought he could find in his head. He expounded on apples, apple trees, apple seeds, clouds, worms, stones, dirt, toenails, beards, and lint.

He was about to air his thoughts on roof shingles when he found the pig farmer had walked away.

With no one to talk to, the farmer went home with nothing in his basket and nothing in his head, and sat down at the kitchen table until it grew dark outside.

Bored and hungry, the farmer went to bed.

The next morning the farmer found
Give curled up and snoring in the basket.

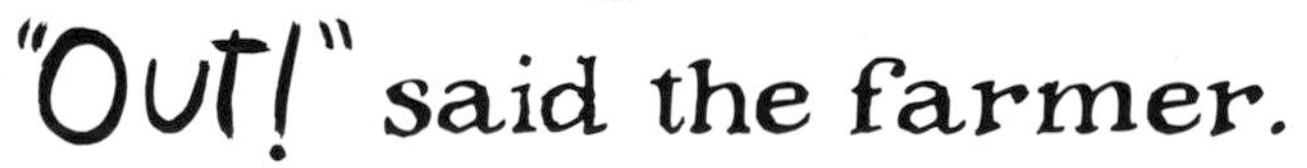

"OUT!" said the farmer.

“Let us go inspect the apples,” said the farmer to his dog. As he added the last apple to his basket beneath the greenest tree in the orchard, he heard a noise.

The two little men were wrestling in the long grass, arguing loudly about who was greater, Give or Take.

Sometimes Give was on top and Take was on the bottom, and sometimes it was the other way around.

Seeing them gave the farmer an idea. He grabbed both of the tiny little men by their collars and put them on top of his apples.

Passing the pumpkins and the pigs, the farmer stopped at the miller's mill. In the basket the little men shouted at each other (and into the farmer's ear), "Take is better!" "Give is better!" "Take!" "Give!"

"Give!" "Take!"

The farmer greeted the miller and said, "May I give you some of my apples and take some of your flour?"

"Fine," said the miller.

"Let me give you some advice," said the farmer. "Make applesauce."

"Take my advice," said the miller. "Make dough."

On the way home the two little men continued to argue. "Take!" "Give!" "Give!" "Take!"

"Hearing them gives me another idea," said the farmer.

As he arrived home, the farmer took some apples for sauce and some flour for dough and put them together.

He put what he had made into the oven and gave it some time to bake.

Soon the farmer smelled a wonderful aroma. When he peeked into the oven, he discovered something new and marvelous—

—an apple pie!

"Sweet," said the farmer. "This is fine. Let us eat our apple pie."

At last, exhausted from their fighting, the two little men looked at each other.

"Take my hand," said the one.

"Give me a hug," said the other.

And then the farmer, his dog, and Give and Take ate the apple pie.

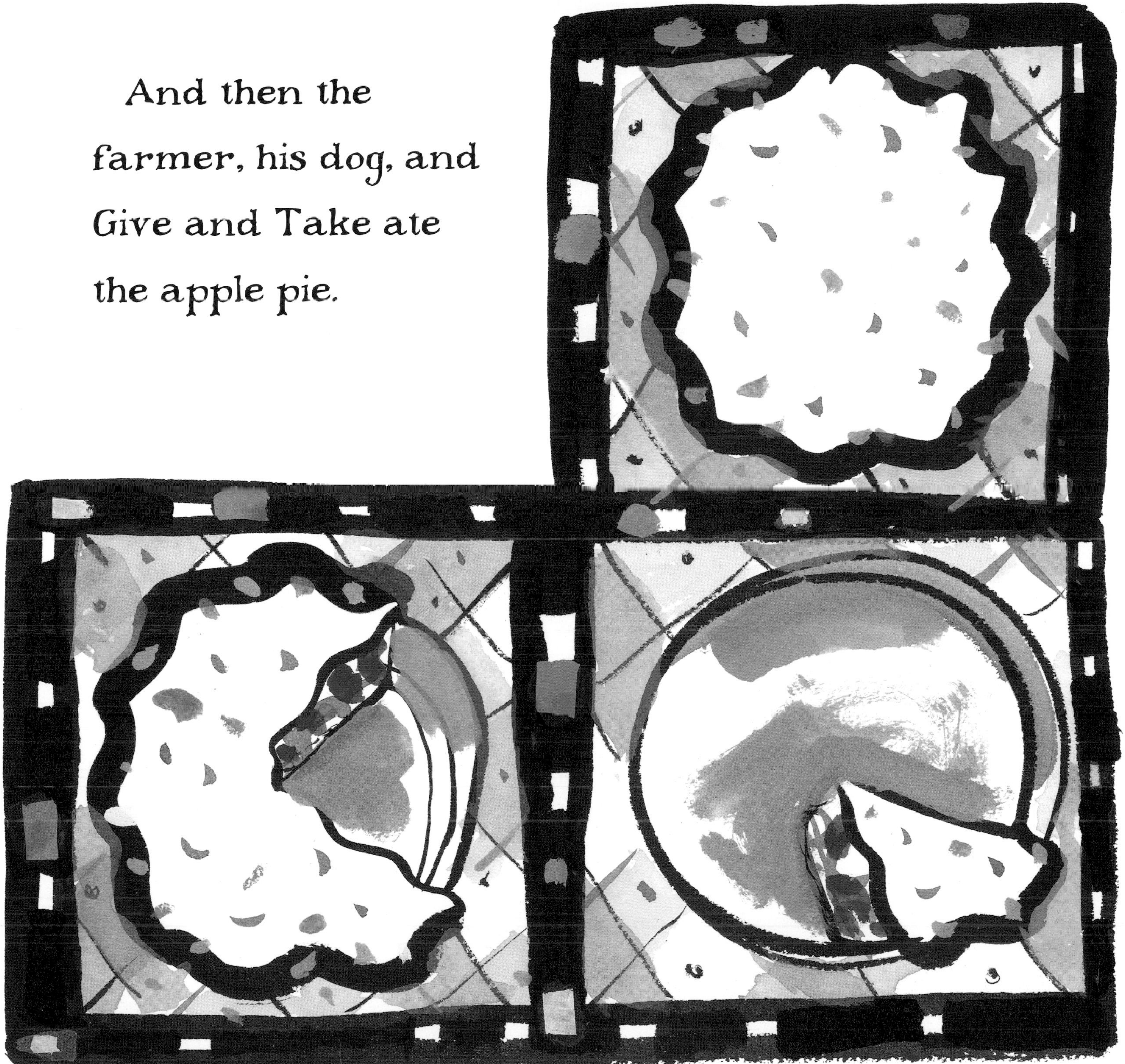